The Great
STORM WHALE

Everyone has a story to tell.
This book is for my mum.

The more things change,
the more they stay the same
Alphonse Karr

SIMON & SCHUSTER
First published in Great Britain in 2023 by Simon & Schuster UK Ltd, 1st Floor, 222 Gray's Inn Road, London WC1X 8HB • Text and illustrations copyright © 2023 Benji Davies • The right of Benji Davies to be identified as the author and illustrator of this work has been asserted by him in accordance with the Copyright, Designs and Patents Act, 1988 • All rights reserved, including the right of reproduction in whole or in part in any form • A CIP catalogue record for this book is available from the British Library upon request • Printed in China • ISBN: 978-1-3985-0349-6 (HB) ISBN: 978-1-3985-0350-2 (PB) • ISBN: 978-1-3985-0351-9 (eBook) • ISBN: 978-1-3985-2873-4 (eAudio) • 10 9 8 7 6 5 4 3 2 1

The Great STORM WHALE

Benji Davies

SIMON & SCHUSTER
London   New York   Sydney   Toronto   New Delhi

Noi lived with his dad and six cats by the sea.
It was autumn and Grandma had come to visit.

Storms were coming. Noi thought of the whale he had once saved from a storm; how he and his dad had helped it back to its family in the sea.

That night the wind howled and Noi could not sleep.

"Let me tell you a story . . ." said Grandma.

"There was once a girl," she began, "who lived on an island. She knew that place like a whale knows every barnacle on its back. And she once met a whale like you did, Noi.

They were good friends – *great* friends.

Her grandpa had made her a wooden flute which she would play to the whale, and the whale would sing back.

The whale came every summer.

But then, one year . . . it didn't."

"What did the girl do,
Grandma?" Noi asked.

"She waited and she waited.
Every day she sat upon the rocks.

Still the whale didn't come.

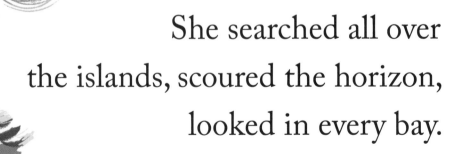

She searched all over
the islands, scoured the horizon,
looked in every bay.

Then, one night, there was a great, wild storm. The girl
didn't want to leave, but her family knew it wasn't safe to stay.

As quickly as they could, they left for higher ground.
Then, through the storm, they saw a light –
a big lightship!

It was there to carry the islanders to safety.

All of their neighbours were on board.
They sang old songs and kept each other warm.

Even so, the girl's home was gone. All of their things,
her wooden flute! Everything had been swept away."

"*Then* what did they do?" asked Noi.

"They had to find a new island, start again.

The girl always wondered if her whale went back to the old island and found that she wasn't there.

Then, one day, something washed up on the shore.

It looked ... familiar.

She found more!

First, cups and plates …
then pieces of wood,
then chairs and coffee pots …

Day by day, all the things from
their old home turned up
on the new island."

Noi sat up. "They just washed up on the shore?" he asked.

"Well, that's what she wondered too – how?

So one morning she woke early and went to find out.

As she walked along the shore, something caught
her eye, glistening in the sand.

It was her wooden flute!

And when she looked up, her whale was there too.
It had brought its whole family.

The whales had found the pieces of her home amongst the waves, and on the bottom of the ocean, and bit by bit they had been bringing them back to her.

Some of it couldn't be used, but piece by piece they built a new house from the old. They made it better – stronger!"

"Is it still there now?"
asked Noi.

Grandma smiled. "Yes, Noi. It's this house –
your house by the sea!"

"And the little girl?" said Noi.

"The little girl was me," said Grandma.
"It was all many, *many* storms ago."

All was calm around Noi's house.

They had fallen fast asleep but when Noi and Grandma woke, they went out to walk along the shore.

Grandma took something from her pocket.
"Noi, this belongs to you now," she said.

It was the wooden flute.

Noi hugged Grandma very tight.

"I think our whales must be from the same family,
Grandma, like we are."

"Yes, Noi," said Grandma with a smile.
"I think that they must be too."

And whenever Noi played that wooden flute . . .

. . . the whales would sing.